I0456664

All I Want for Christmas is a

MARINE

TARA NINA

All I Want for Christmas is a Marine

By

Tara Nina

Please be advised this book was previously published in 2009.
It has been revised prior to current release.
All rights reserved
Copyright© 2019 by Tara Nina
Cover Art by Syneca of OriginalSyn
Published by T.N.Books
ISBN ebook: 978-1-7342057-1-8

This book is licensed for individual readership only. No portion of this book may be resold or redistributed in any format by any means, electronic or mechanical, including photocopying, recording, or by any information storage and retrieval system without expressed written consent of the author. If you would like to share this book with another person, please purchase an additional copy for each person. Thank you for respecting the author's work.

This is a work of fiction. Names, characters and events are creations of the author's imagination. Any resemblance to any persons, living or dead, is purely coincidental and unintentional by the author.

To obtain permission to excerpt portions of the text, please contact the author at http://taranina.com

T.N.Books
New Jersey
2018

Published in the USA

Chapter One

Rain dripped in his eyes, but he never lost sight of the objective. In and out. That was the plan. Locate, identify, observe, and report that's what Staff Sergeant Mitch Sinclair's squad of Force Recon Marines did best. Their assignment had been to uncover the truth of Kim Jong-il's health. Was he dead or gravely ill? Rumors contaminated the media. At 0800 hours, their mission changed from green ops—collect intelligence—to black ops—direct action. Separated from returning to their battalion by a sudden surge of North Korean militant action, they adapted to the situation.

Now, their job entailed extraction of the daughter of an American scientist from the North Korean's. With the way the North Korean leader, Kim Jong-il hated Americans, Mitch found it ironic the dictator's youngest son, Kim Jong-un, ordered the capture of an American in order to help their cause. The attempt to kidnap David Summers, creator of the highly classified MD-3 missile navigation system, failed. So instead, they took Summers' daughter to use as leverage to gain the knowledge they desperately needed to back their nuclear claims. Intelligence out of P'yongyang helped thwart the scientist's capture, but it came too late to prevent Jong-un's back-up plan. Take the only child of a widowed eccentric scientist and hold her hostage in exchange for missile guidance technology.

What the North Korean's didn't know...Allie Summers was the key to unlock that information. Due to her father's high level of intelligence, he lacked focus without her at his side. That little bit of information, Mitch hoped the enemy never discovered. If they did...he sighed heavily. He hated to think what they'd do to her to obtain the secrets they wanted. Torture was a way of life for these militant groups and the North Korean's held the charter on nasty techniques. This he'd learned from studying the Korean War and listening to stories from his uncles who were there. He never thought he'd be following in their footsteps in another *disagreement* with North Korea. This time the issue was nuclear.

Hopefully, he prayed, North Korea would back down from the pressure of strict sanctions from the UN. A smidgeon of doubt about Kim Jong-il's sanity and health clouded that hope. From everything Mitch read, this dictator lacked the foresight to understand the repercussions of using nuclear weapons. Everyone suffered from the fall out and not just the country fired upon.

Now, because of this lunatic, Mitch and his squad were in North Korea's mountainous terrain watching and waiting for the perfect moment to strike. Part of him hungered for the chance to take out a few of the enemy, but the good Recon Marine in him knew his job. Get in and out without being seen or firing a shot and save the hostage from harm. Forty-eight hours was a long time to be captive. If he could help it, tonight would be her last night as a victim.

A pair of dark brown eyes haunted him. The picture of Allie Summers seemed tattooed inside his head. Something about those big, brown eyes captured him the moment he studied her file. Mitch swiped the back of his hand across his eyes removing the excess water from the driving rain. Returning his gaze to the practically non-detectable camouflaged building in the distance, he waited and watched for the chance to complete this mission.

From a smattering of intercepted coded conversations, Mitch and his men gathered the fact a package was due for delivery. The low rumble of an engine cut through the steady pound of the rain. Mitch slid his night vision goggles in place and studied the unmarked panel van make its way along the narrow dirt road. When it came to a stop, six men exited the building and surrounded the van.

* * * * * * *

Bounced around in the back of a cold vehicle, Allie struggled with her bindings. Pain burned into her wrists and sizzled up her cramped arms. Both feet were numb and she ached to wiggle them, but she'd long since lost the ability to even move her toes. Wrapped in a dirty burlap sack, she couldn't see. Slivers of light snuck through the tiny weaves of the fabric informing her when day turned to night. From her calculations, she'd been in this bag for roughly forty-eight to fifty hours. With the ability to roll around, she assumed she was in the back of a van or cargo truck of some sort.

The gag in her mouth prevented her from speech or swallowing. Desert dryness coated her tongue making her hunger for water. The sound of rain pound the roof of the moving vehicle almost made her laugh. If not for the gag, she would have. A torrential downpour outside and not one drop for her to drink.

Eyes closed, she tried to make sense of the past two days. How had she gotten here? One minute she was stepping out of a cab to represent her father at a scientific awards ceremony, the next she was here. From the dialect she'd heard, she determined her capturers were of Asian descent. An eerie sensation in the pit of her stomach suggested she wasn't in the States anymore. Somehow they'd managed to smuggle her out. But to where? And Why?

Then it hit her. An image flashed inside her brain of a recent news break she'd watched. North Korea...oh God, had she been taken by the North Korean's? The vehicle halted. Rain poured outside. The doors opened and shut on the vehicle's front. Somewhere close, another door opened. Heavy footsteps fell. Allie strained to hear, but couldn't decipher the voices. Did they know the truth?

Inhaling deep through her nostrils didn't ease the sudden knot in her chest. It only managed to fill her lungs with stale air and induced the need to cough. Fear gripped her system, but she refused to relinquish command to such weakness. She needed strength to think straight. Focusing on her father, she gathered a calm from deep within her soul and willed her senses to right. *Think*, she reprimanded. How could they have discovered she was the driving force behind her father's ideas? No one knew. She made certain over the past few years to cover their family secret from scrutiny. He'd fallen apart when mother died. To protect her father's reputation, she stepped into her mother's shoes as his assistant and helped keep her father's gifted intelligence on track.

No one knew she'd done more than assist. She worked closely with him on this latest system. Being the daughter of a genius had its perks *and* its downfalls. As a child, she hated being the smartest kid in class so her parents shielded her from the hurt and home schooled her. Through a variety of online colleges, she earned several different masters degrees, one of which was nuclear physics.

There wasn't a schematic in this guidance system she didn't understand since she helped create the design.

There's no way the Koreans knew. She made father promise not to state the extent of her participation in this project in his documentation. The memory of that disagreement brought momentary joy to her heart. He wanted to share acknowledgement of the accomplishment with her, but she refused, convincing him her time to shine in the scientific world would eventually come. She wanted him to remain billed as one of America's top scientists until the day he died and she didn't care how much of her work went into keeping him at the top. In truth, she feared losing him. He guided and pushed her forward, urged her to propel into new venues of science. Without him…

Allie bit against the gag in her mouth hoping to somehow chew through it, but couldn't. Each movement of her hands dug the binding deeper into her wrists, instead of loosening it.

There had to be a way to escape. She needed to get back to her father and make sure he was safe. Without him, she'd be lost and alone. Together, they were a brilliant team. Moisture coated her cheek as a tear rolled from the corner of her eye. He was all she had left.

Her eyes widened as the thought struck. Did they have him too?

Panic thrashed her system. She had to get out of here and find him. He had to be safe. Breathe, she reminded herself. Now was not the time to hyperventilate. In, out, slow and easy, she forced herself to inhale and exhale until her nerves settled. If her father was in danger, she'd need her wits about her to think things through and get them out of here.

Allie lay still listening to the rain and straining to hear the voices of her captures. Male, distinctively male. A loud grate of metal upon metal broke the air. The doors of the rear of the vehicle opened. Cool wind blew in causing her to shiver. A foreign tongue echoed as a hand clasped her ankle. With no regard to her safety or comfort, he dragged her across the floor to the door. Bumped and bruised she managed to hold her head up to keep it from bouncing on the hardness, desperately trying to prevent being knocked unconscious.

Cold steel touched her skin and she stilled. Tightness left her ankles the moment he sliced the ropes. One shoe on and one shoe off, they drug her from the van to stand. Silence filled her ears echoed by the steady beat of rain on the ground, the van and the canvas bag secluding her from view. She sensed several stood around her as she struggled on stiff legs to remain upright. The rip of cloth, the sensation of material parting and the occasional nick of the blade made her fully aware they removed the burlap shroud. Blinking, she held her head down until her eyesight adjusted. A fist in her hair jerked her head upward shooting stars behind her eyes. Shifting her weight to her bare foot, Allie attacked the assailant's knee with the other still sporting a six-inch black leather stiletto.

The sudden release of her hair and his simultaneous howl granted her a brief instant of freedom. Running haphazardly, she dodged two men before another tackled her from behind sending them skidding face first in the mud. Before he could get a good grip on her, she twisted and turned trying to escape. With her mouth gagged, she couldn't bite. Both hands still tied tight together she flailed her arms like a club knocking him in the side of the head.

The point of a rifle in her face followed by the heavily accented word, "Halt," caused her to cede in her struggle. The mud-covered man on top of her jumped to his feet. For several long seconds, she lay still, catching her breath and accessing her surroundings. Rain pelted her face washing some of the mud away. It stung her eyes, but she hesitated to wipe them with her dirty, bound hands.

They wanted something from her or else she'd already be dead. Allie swiped the gun barrel out of her face as she sat upright. Covered in thick mud, she struggled without help to her feet. She maintained as much grace and dignity that a one shoed, soaking wet, mud-covered woman could muster, and stared the owner of the gun in the eye.

His silence and steady stare provoked her anger. She was in no mood for any further games. Cold, tired, hungry and though she hated to admit it, fear made her insides quiver. Not relinquishing his stare, she managed to wiggle her fingers under the gag and together with the push of her tongue removed it from her mouth. She caught enough rain to coat her tongue and wet her mouth. Slowly enunciating each word she demanded. "What…do…you…want…with…me?"

"Nothing."

She spun to see a man in the open doorway of a building. He stood several inches shorter than she at roughly five foot even at best, she surmised.

The light positioned behind him gave his lean frame an eerily dark appearance and hid his features from view. Obviously, he was the one in control. Clipped commands in what she suspected as Korean and the men scurried to please. The man with the gun lowered the barrel produced a knife and removed the bindings from her wrists. A man on either side of her nudged her toward the door though she hesitated to move. She simply stared at the shadowed, short man. He sidestepped, keeping his back against the door and waved a hand inward toward the warm, inviting glow of the room.

"For now you shall be treated as my guest."

A solid push from behind and she was forced to close the gap between them. As she stepped into the doorway, he leaned close. His voice turned sinister as he warned.

"Try to escape again and the punishment will be unpleasant."

Faster than she'd ever seen anyone move, he brought the man to her left to his knees with a series of swift blows and showed no mercy when he snapped his neck ending his life. The gasp froze in her throat as the sight of the man she'd stabbed with her shoe crumpled into a heap.

Heated words left his lips and the man was quickly dragged into the night. Her knees threatened to buckle. She'd never seen a man killed and prayed she'd never see it again. Pulling her eyes from the disappearing dead man she stared at their leader. She managed to force one word from her lips.

"Why?"

"It is a weak man who cannot keep a hold on a woman especially one that's bound and gagged. His death proved to the others failure is not tolerated."

He spun on his heels and marched into the room. Not sure whether from fear for her life or the man who nudged her in the side, she followed him into the lighted room. If nothing else, it was warm and dry.

Chapter Two

Mitch couldn't believe his eyes. The woman was long and lethal. A black strappy stiletto caught and held his attention when they slid her from the back of the van. *Sexy* shot through his head for a millisecond before he shoved it from his thoughts. Missing a shoe didn't matter. Her legs were lean and sculpted from what he could see. Inch by slow inch, they cut the burlap sack revealing a beautiful woman. It reminded him of a magic trick.

The skillful placement of her stiletto amazed him and brought a smile to his lips. The woman had style. Dressed in a mid-thigh black evening dress, she handled her capturers with grace and the finesse of a greased pig. They couldn't get a hand on her for a matter of minutes as she did an awkward bob and weave, eluding them in the pouring rain. He bet if she had on a matching set of shoes—or better yet, sneakers—they wouldn't have caught her.

He stiffened at the sight of her being tackled from behind. The pair slid for several feet until they stopped. It didn't faze her. She continued to fight for her freedom. He caught sight of the gun before she did and instinctively placed the man in his cross hairs. One wrong move and he'd drop him where he stood. They'd been instructed to bring her home alive and he planned to complete this mission. He couldn't help but snort heavily when she sat upright and shoved the gun out of her face. Either she was the bravest woman he'd ever seen or she was insane. At the moment, he couldn't decide which.

When she turned toward the open door, he followed her line of sight. *Damn*, he hissed under his breath. Kwan Sung-hee. The worst of the worst stood in the doorway of the building. Short, powerful and deadly. Known for severe torture tactics and brute force. This was not good. Kim

Jong-un employed one of the deadliest and most elusive mercenaries in the world.

Keeping the gun level, he never lost sight of her. Soaking wet and covered in mud, she managed to maintain an air of dignity and defiance. Even at such a distance, he sensed strength radiate off her. The only glitch, she wobbled for a split second when Kwan killed the man he recognized by his limp as the man she'd spiked with her heel. Death was a given in his profession, but he knew it wasn't in hers.

The moment the door closed he lost sight of her. Dread settled in the pit of his stomach. They had to get her out of there as quickly as possible before that monster turned her inside out. Three clicks of his tongue to the sensitive mic inside his highly specialized helmet and he got the information he needed. They were ready at his go. Armed with the latest weaponry, Mitch knew his band of Force Recon Marines were the top in their field. This wasn't the first hostage removal they'd completed.

Switching to thermal heat sensing binoculars, Mitch located and counted the enemy. The dead body lay in the back of the van as one drove it away. Two men patrolled the front of the building while another set of two guarded the back. He located the other two inside the building along with Kwan and Miss Summers. No, he chided himself. Never give the package a name. It turned the mission personal and that wasn't allowed. Shaking off his momentary lapse in marine judgment, he relayed the info to his brothers.

Once he knew they each understood, they waited for the right moment to pounce undetected and recover the hostage. But for how long? How long would she survive should Kwan decide to interrogate her by way of one of his horrendous methods?

Moments later, the hostage was led to a room on the far back right corner of the building.

Obviously, they locked her in. What happened next stilled the air in his lungs. It appeared as if she undressed. Every ounce of moisture dried in his mouth. It wasn't right to watch, but he couldn't help it. From her movements, he knew she entered a shower. Though he tired not to, his eyes glued to her actions for several long seconds before the dedicated marine in him reminded him he had a job to do. Mitch swallowed hard as he readjusted the sudden tautness of his balls. Never had he reacted to anyone as he did to her, especially while on duty.

The sound of a throat clear whispered through the built-in headset of his helmet jerking him back to reality and let him know he wasn't the only one aware of her actions. Every man on this mission was equipped to the hilt with the latest computer enhanced gadgetry. They saw what he saw. Heat filtered up his spine. For a reason he couldn't explain he didn't like that fact.

Mitch closed his eyes for a split second, took a deep breath and cleared his head. *Think mission and nothing else.* Extract package, return it safely to base, submit report and return to the field. That was the way of his world. It didn't include a woman. Not now, not ever.

Opening his eyes, he caught sight of the guard's movement. One remained at each door while each of the other two rotated. While a man walked to the left and around to the front the other walked to the right and rounded to the back. Glancing at the time, he realized it happened at exactly fifteen minutes from when they'd taken their posts. Perfect, he let a slight smile tug at his lips. If they did it again, it would be their downfall.

Within minutes his men were in place. They knew their jobs. Take down the guard they were assigned without making a sound or being seen. Not a problem. Exactly fifteen minutes passed and the guards rotated. The instant each turned the corner; they hit the ground with a silent thud. The men located at the front and back door were silenced as well. Mitch wasted no time. He entered through the window of the room where she was held.

Looking into the open bathroom, he froze. She stood wrapped in a towel. Moisture glistened her skin. He knew the moment she spotted him. Her eyes widened and he reacted quickly. He couldn't let her scream.

* * * * * * *

Both legs trembled, but she refused to let her captor see her fear. He killed a man in cold blood. Would he do the same to her? Swallowing hard, she didn't doubt it. One, two, three she counted each step trying to calm her nerves. When he turned to face her, she stopped, tilted her chin and straightened her spine. Even though she leaned wearing only one stiletto, she grappled for an ounce of dignity and hoped she portrayed a siren calm collected manner she truly didn't feel inside.

To level her gaze on his, she lowered her chin. At five foot seven inches tall, she towered over him. Yep, she was right. He barely cleared five foot. In his case, height didn't matter. She'd witnessed his deadly capabilities first hand. Though heavily accented with an Asian flair, his English was well pronounced.

"Miss Summers, as long as you are here you will be considered my guest. I have taken it upon myself to make you as comfortable as possible. My men have been informed to *protect* you by any means."

The gleam in his eyes sent a cold chill down her spine. His attempt at a smile gave her the willies. It wasn't full-toothed or happy. It twisted more like a sinister grin; speaking volumes of the pain he knew how to inflict rather than easing her nerves and making her comfortable. Gathering as much salvia as possible, she managed to speak on a grated whisper.

"Why am I here?" Uncontrollable shivers set in, causing her to rub her arms against the chill.

"You are cold." He grabbed her elbow and it was all she could do not to pull away. "Let me show you to your room."

Refusing to move at his attempt to guide her, she stated again. "Why am I here?"

His eyes narrowed, but she maintained a slim grasp on her fear keeping it buried beneath the surface. After several seconds of silence and staring at her as if scrutinizing her intelligence, he spoke.

"You are a mere pawn in a much bigger game."

"You're after my father." She stated bluntly not wavering from his intimidating glare.

"Intelligent as you are beautiful," he released her arm, but continued to walk as if they were having a casual conversation. She followed. "Your father has something my employer wants."

"What makes you think that?"

"Don't play coy with me, Miss Summers. Your father created a missile guidance system which is worth far more the United States government has given him."

"My father is a patriot," she stiffened. "He believes in his country."

"Do you? Are you willing to die if he refuses to exchange the information for your life?"

"I trust my father."

"Then for your sake," he sneered as he stopped and opened the door on the far right side of the room. "Let us hope he makes the right choice."

Allie opened her mouth to speak, but closed it instead.

"Your room, Miss Summers. You will find a bathroom complete with toiletries. Also, a change of clothes can be found laid out for you on the bed." The touch of his hand down the back of her gown to her waist made her involuntarily flinch. "Of course, it is nothing to match the finest silk which you wear. Too bad the rain and your attempted escape ruined it. Do not try that again. It would be a shame to preempt your life before its time. There are armed guards surrounding the building. While you refresh, I shall see to your nourishment."

The moment the door closed, she heard the distinct sound of the lock. There was no getting out that way. She scurried to the window, glanced from side to side, but saw nothing. It too was locked from the outside. Caged like a lab rat, she huffed. Dried crusted mud made her itch. Coldness settled deep into her flesh making her shake from head to toe. She needed to think, but at this rate hypothermia would probably set in before she managed to engage her brain.

Allie walked into the bathroom and noted there was no door. It contained the basic needs, a shower surrounded by a wooden stall, a toilet and a sink. Nothing fancy. Simple bar soap sat on the sink. A toothbrush and toothpaste, a comb, a towel, a washcloth and a roll of toilet paper rounded out the amenities of this no-star establishment. She huffed at her attempt at humor. She doubted this place existed on any of the Internet vacation booking sites. When she started the shower, she realized there was no shampoo so she grabbed the bar of soap from the sink.

As quick as she could, she peeled the dress and her undergarments from her skin. Wiggling out of her single stiletto, she frowned. That was the best set of leather shoes she'd ever owned. She opened the creaky wooden door and stepped into the shower. Not comfortable without the ability to lock the bathroom for privacy, she quickly scrubbed the mud from her hair and body. There was no way she intended to be caught naked if that midget of a maniac decided to pay another visit before she dressed. Every muscle ached, causing her to linger longer than she should have in the heated water. Tears ran down her cheeks.

God, she prayed father was all right. From the sound of it, he wasn't a captive. Only she was a prisoner. That thought released a smidgeon of the knot in her gut. Hopefully, his sister, Myra, would remain with him until she returned. *If she returned*, she wiped the tears from her eyes and shut the water off. Tears equaled weakness and she refused to yield to that bodily function again. Not until she was home.

Allie stepped from the shower, dried then wrapped in the towel. She ran the comb through her hair, brushed her teeth then stilled. Did she hear something? A quick turn of the knob and the water flow to the sink stopped. Straining, she heard nothing. She turned, walked into the bedroom and froze.

A man clad from head to toe in American military camouflage and heavily armed stood staring at her. Before she could speak, he moved lightning fast. A hand covered her mouth while the other tugged her close from behind.

"Sush," his warm breath tickled her ear. But his deep, southern drawl touched her in other places making her shiver as he continued to whisper. "I'm Staff Sergeant Mitch Sinclair with the Marines, ma'am and we're here to take you home."

Allie bit his hand lightly, causing him to jerk it free from her mouth. She twisted in his grip, grappling for the towel that had loosened, leveled her gaze on his and whispered on a hurried breath.

"I can see that. Give me a second to dress and I'm out that window behind you."

Without giving him a chance, she shrugged from his grip, dropped the towel and lunged for the clothes on the bed. She tugged on the sweatshirt and sweatpants without bothering with the undergarments. Grabbing the socks, she noticed there were no shoes so she tossed them back on the bed.

Mitch's jaw dropped. The most perfectly rounded bottom stood within arms length and he couldn't do a thing about it. He spun on his heels, weapon drawn and guarded the door while she dressed. *Think mission. Think bad guys. Think Kwan.*

That did it. Pure heat sizzled up his spine to curl in his gut. Images of some of the grisly innocent deaths that had befallen at that man's hand flashed inside his head, chilling the unwanted sensation of desire. But not for long. She touched his shoulder and he turned to face her. Deep, brown eyes framed by wet golden hair melted his soul.

"No shoes," she whispered.

"It'll have to do. Let's get you out of here first."

Mitch cautiously peeked through the open window. With a nod, Sergeant Lou Randle appeared on the other side. He helped the hostage through the window then followed. As his feet touched ground, he noted the undergarments still lay on the bed. Knowing she wore nothing under those sweats sent a spike of need straight to his loins. What was wrong with him?

A knock on the door jarred him into combat stance as he backed away from the building. The moment they hit the woods, Kwan Sung-hee discovered he no longer held Allie Summers captive.

"Find her. Kill her," echoed behind them in heated Korean. Mitch had no intention of allowing that to happen.

Chapter Three

Lou took point of the four-man team, leading the way through the thick trees. Radio controller, Sergeant Eric Wise fell in behind Lou. Sergeant Dean Richards brought up the rear making sure the enemy didn't engage. Even with the woven canopy of branches and leaves, rain pelted them. Mitch followed Allie making sure she didn't fall. Bare feet made her slip and slide through the torrential downpour. Though she didn't complain, Mitch knew the wooded terrain and underbrush attacked her tender feet. He shifted his weapon to hang easily accessible across his chest. Matching her shorter strides, he strode beside her just in time to catch her when her foot caught on a root.

"Thank you," she managed to whisper.

"Not a problem, ma'am," he scooped an arm under her knees and wrapped the other around her waist, tugging her against his weapon and his chest. She gasped. Both arms laced around his neck as if frightened he'd drop her. A smile threatened his lips, but he swallowed it. He bench-pressed three times her weight. There was no way he'd drop something as light as this hot morsel. Awareness of her feminine essence captivated his system. Light as a feather and soft temptation gathered against him cradled in his arms. Visions of her naked bottom flashed behind his eyes as he readjusted his grip. Thinking of her like that was wrong. He reprimanded his libido to back down, took a breath and forced a natural even tone. "We've a long distance to cover. It's too difficult to do without shoes and keep pace."

"I…" the retort stopped dead in her throat.

"You managed about a quarter mile bare foot. Leave the rest to me."

As if she'd accepted her fate as his burden to carry, she leaned into him no longer fighting the predicament. He sensed her exhaustion as she lowered her head onto his shoulder and closed her eyes. Dean whipped out a neatly folded, camouflaged rain poncho from his side pack pocket.

"This might help warm her some," he claimed, draping it over her like a blanket, tucking it in around her.

Each tuck of the poncho tightened her presence in his arms. His intent had been simply to increase their pace and alleviate any further damage to her feet. The discomfort in his chest had nothing to do with the dig of his weapon into his flesh and everything to do with the woman in his arms.

"You done," Mitch stated in a point-blank tone.

"Thank you." Allie mumbled from beneath the cocoon of rain resistant nylon.

"You're welcome, ma'am," Dean touched the brim of his combat helmet, shot Mitch a raised eyebrow told-you-so look then fell into place guarding the rear.

Hours past and the rain didn't let up. He was grateful for the unusual warmth in the late November climate. Otherwise, no matter what gear they wore, they'd be fighting hypothermia. Clutching her close, Mitch and his men forged through the woods and kept moving south at a steady pace. With the persistent downfall, he knew the odds of flash floods in this region increased. The trek to the Imjin River consisted of miles of treacherous terrain downhill. During the rainy season, the river was prone to torrential currents yet he knew it would be their greatest chance of escape. It had been their main entrance into North Korea without being seen and if luck remained at his side, it'd be their exit without incident.

Crossing the Demilitarized zone and entering Yonch'on, South Korea was their only hope of refuge. Captain Hayward waited in at the base camp set-up outside Yonch'on for word of their mission. There would be no formal military action to rescue Mitch and his men should they fall under fire or capture. Their top-secret objective warranted no scrutiny from the press. The outside world would not know of their victory or failure. It was the way of the Force Recon Marine. Knowing they'd completed their mission successfully equaled the only glory Mitch required. For fifteen years, the Marine Corps had been his life, his reason to live.

Holding the phenomenal length of woman in his arms, his world seemed to hunger for a new direction. Mitch glanced at the sleeping beauty. Her lips pursed in a slight pout as if begging for a kiss. Thick eyelashes fluttered for an instant and he sensed she dreamt. The sudden twitch of facial movements led him to believe a nightmare tormented her rest. Before he could stop himself, he leaned in and whispered.

"Rest, Allie. You're safe. I promise no-ones going to harm you." Not sure why he did it, he brushed a gentle kiss across her furrowed brow. The momentary touch caused his mouth to water and increased his desire to taste her lips to their fullest. The insatiable need jolted him upright, straightened his spine taut and instinctively tightened his grip around his precious prize.

Oh god, he prayed silently. *Give me the strength to complete my mission and walk away to live another day as a Marine.*

* * * * * * *

Allie started to balk when he first lifted her into his arms. She was an independent woman and needed no assistance in walking or running for that matter. Exhaustion gripped her system overriding her normal strong-willed attitude. The ache in her legs and the sting of multiple slender cuts to the bottoms of her feet aided in her decision to accept his help. The pit of her stomach heated when he shifted her close and carried her like a damsel in distress. Out of the two men she'd dated, neither ever lifted her much less treated her as delicately as this big, tough Marine.

This was a man she'd enjoy getting to know. She shivered, trying to prevent her mind from wandering in a non-professional direction. Apparently, saving her was his team's mission. Nothing more, nothing less. It wouldn't do to let her imagination create an incorrect scenario. But her hormones whipped along at a rapid pace, twisting her thoughts back to the romantic.

Was there a hint of an underlying warning in the way he snapped *'you done'* at his fellow soldier? Nah, she decided. Even though she'd sensed an electric spark from her head to her toes the moment she laid eyes on him, she doubted he'd experienced the same. Camouflage didn't hide the healthy male specimen from her trained eye. Without the dark face paint, she bet chiseled features surrounded his set of sexy, bright blue eyes. The helmet hid the color of his hair making her itch to unravel that mystery by removing it.

And if he smiled, she'd probably melt. Thank God he didn't smile, she retorted mentally.

The steel of his weapon lay between them digging into her side and hip. Though it bit into her comfort she was grateful for the cold barrier it placed between them. Without it, she wasn't certain she wouldn't embarrass herself by snuggling tighter against this massive machine of a man. They'd walked for miles and yet he showed no signs of fatigue. His fortitude astounded her and kept her libido ramped on high, even though she tried desperately to tone it down. The rhythm of his gait lulled her to sleep in the sanctity of his arms.

For now, she was safe.

Deep sleep wasn't possible, but a catnap engulfed her system though she tried to fight the inevitable. Bumped and bruised tossed around wrapped in a burlap sack, hours dissipated lost forever. Rain poured, mouth dried. Visions of a strange man's face danced behind her eyes. His macabre smile tormented her soul. Eyes filled with a history of torture, resentment and hate gazed directly at her as if daring her to run. Tiny hands twisted a man's head, snapping his neck, sealing his fate. Her chest constricted. The gasp froze in her throat.

Would she be next?

Refusing to open her eyes for fear of seeing the short little man with the deadly skills, Allie stiffened against the cold hard steel.

A warm breath touched her ear. Whispered words of comfort unknotted the coil wrapped tight around her chest, allowing her to breath with ease. Whether intentional or not, the cradle of his arms cuddled her closer, coaxing her system to relax. The realization she was no longer held captive emerged from her sleep-induced haze. The brush of masculine lips across her brow sealed the need to get to know this man better. He knew nothing of her and she of him, but deep in her heart, the desire to learn and explore his attributes ignited.

If she thought too hard about it, she'd convince herself she suffered from some sort of hero worship syndrome. After all, he had rescued her. His sudden stop stirred her from the momentary haven of safety. Muffled noises sounded in the distance.

Allie peeked from beneath the rain poncho and whispered, "Where are we?"

His brilliant blues met hers and for a split second she thought he'd kiss her. *Wrong.* Instead, he communicated the need for silence with a shake of his head. Damn the romantic notion. This man was all business. She swallowed hard. Considering the situation, she knew she needed to remain level headed and listen to these highly trained specialists, if she wanted to survive. Instinctively, she followed his lead and lowered to her feet. Instant coldness replaced the warmth he'd given her causing her to internally shiver. The moment she had her balance, he readied his weapon and shifted into a combat stance keeping her close behind. She placed each step carefully in the indention of his boot print in the mud.

Where he stepped, she stepped.

It took great inner strength to resist the temptation to kiss her. Those sleepy, dark brown eyes of hers relayed desire mixed with fear. And fear was an emotion he refused to touch. He'd already made a wrong move by kissing her brow. The salt of her skin left a flavor sealed to his lips he would never forget. The essence was pure Allie, an intelligent woman with an air of refined innocence.

Her file read like an encyclopedia of knowledge and achievements. The woman he protected maintained a high IQ, not to mention several master's degrees in Science, Math, Art and the one that worried him the most, Nuclear Physics. Did Kwon know that? If he did, there'd be no way he'd give up on such a prized commodity easily. Her value to the mercenary would triple. Mitch knew Kwon would torture her to extract every ounce of information he could then either sell it or her or both to the highest bidder. Kwon knew no loyalty to any employer.

The low rumble of off road vehicles seemed to hover within a half-mile radius. It surprised him they used quads for mobility. But given the tough terrain, it seemed a logical choice. For the last hour, the engines groan echoed through the trees from several different directions behind them. Mitch gave thanks for the rain. Though it slowed their return to the location where they hid their boat, it also covered their tracks and hampered Kwan's progress as well. The night before they travelled up river via high speed, silent motorized inflatable boat. The hike up mountain through thick, wooded terrain hadn't fazed his well-trained Marines. One glance over his shoulder and he read the fatigue in her eyes. She looked lost in the oversized rain poncho. And he knew her bare feet took a beating. Allie didn't have the physical stamina or hours of military training under her belt he did. This wore on her and seeing that touched a soft spot in his heart. She needed him. Mitch forced his gaze back to scanning the area. With the cover of the storm, Mitch hoped they'd still be able to access the boat and the river without being seen.

Lou's whispered warning through the communications system in their helmets made his jaw clench. Now, they had a new threat. A band of North Korean militant's camped blocking the most direct route to the Imjin River. They'd have to work their way around, but it wouldn't be easy. On Lou's cue, Erick took point and they switched to a due east heading giving the camp a broad radius. Lou shifted to the rear, keeping watch with Dean making sure no movement came from the militants. Allie stayed within the tight net of Marines as they increased their pace. The sooner they got out of range of that group the better.

It didn't take long before the roar of engines entered the camp behind them. Angry voices echoed through the trees. Mitch strained to hear picking out a few words from the wind. Shouted commands knotted his gut. Kwan had a connection with these militants. His orders filled the woods with vigilantes armed with guns searching for Allie and whoever helped her escape. Bodies crashed through the underbrush and the rumble of off road quads let them know the hunt escalated, tipping the scales in Kwan's favor.

Though Allie didn't complain, he caught sight of her wince with every footfall and knew her feet were badly damaged. Mitch stopped short, turned and caught Allie before she ran head first into him. On a hoarse whisper, he commanded.

"We've got to move faster. Piggy back, now."

He turned and stooped before her, cutting a darkened gaze across his shoulder at her. The snap of a limb nearby made Allie jump. She didn't hesitate. She hoisted onto his back, wrapped her legs tight around his waist, hooked her feet together and grasped his shoulders. Mitch made one quick adjustment to the added weight, but never released his weapon. It was up to her to hold on. The team fell into combat ready mode as they hustled through the trees, trying to place distance between them and the enemy without giving their location away.

The heat of him between her legs warded off the chill of the ice-cold rain. She knew they must look ridiculous racing through the woods as if they were kids playing a game of chicken in a pool. Drenched as she was she could have easily been in a pool. An image of Staff Sergeant Mitch Sinclair wearing a bathing suit kicked up the heat in her veins. Allie would have smiled if the situation weren't so dire. Ominous echoes reverberated through the trees reminding her, death followed on their heels.

Closer and closer the engines hummed. Branches cracked. Voices carried angry shouts she could only imagine equaled her demise. Her heart beat in her throat and she readjusted her grip to lace her arms around his neck, pulling her snug against him. The man beneath her didn't falter. Neither did the band of men around them. Each movement in-sync with the other like a magical military dance awed her. Her life lay in their refined capabilities.

The rise and fall of his breathing against her chest caused an unexpected reaction. Allie tried to prevent it by clenching her abdominal muscles and sucking in tight, but it failed. Both nipples pebbled with each brush against his back. God, she hoped he hadn't felt them before arching her shoulders, placing a gap between them. A thin layer of cool filled the slender space. It didn't help. Instead, she shivered involuntarily scraping the taut renegades across his shoulder blades. If they were any sharper they'd have cut through both their clothing. That thought almost made her giggle, but she managed to swallow it. It had to be the total exhaustion making her giddy, she decided. Allie buried her head behind his and struggled for control over these sudden surges of uncontrollable bodily reactions. It wasn't in her normal to visibly react this way.

On a heavy sigh, she determined it had to be the extreme circumstances for this overreaction. At least that's what the analytical side of her brain tried to convince the hopeless romantic in her soul. Fear thrashed through her system with each noise closing in on their proximity. Allie clawed tighter to his neck, but quickly loosened her grip when he flexed letting her know she choked him.

She wanted to whisper sorry, but didn't dare break the silence. They moved like creatures of the night. Hand signals and occasional clicks of their tongues were their main mode of communication at this point with the enemy closing in. Eric brought them to a halt. Several feet ahead, water roared its way down the mountain like a giant water slide.

Mitch stood rigid on the bank of what twenty-four hours earlier had been a minor stream, which fed into the Imjin River. With the torrential rain, it now was a rapid flowing tributary. A decision needed to be made. Continue winding down along the bank or use this new fast paced waterway to their advantage. He knew he and his men could navigate it without a problem. But Allie, he doubted she'd make it without help.

As if they'd read his mind, Eric, Lou and Dean were quickly making their gear watertight. Mitch helped Allie to her feet. The glide of her body down his sent an arrow of need straight to his balls. Never had he reacted in such a manner to a woman. Usually, they were a temporary ornament in his life then they were gone the moment they got too serious. Something about this one piqued more than just his interest. The brush of her nipples with each step he had taken weakened his resolve to do his duty, uphold his oath and not ravish the beauty on his back. Did she realize what she did to him? He cupped her chin as he placed a finger to his lips. Her nod relayed her compliance. The look in her eyes made him doubt she understood the full strength of her feminine wiles. Pure innocence stared back at him for a second before he turned and quickly waterproofed his gear as best as possible. The rain soaked everything, but what they didn't need were their weapons becoming waterlogged while body surfing downstream.

Mitch took Allie's hand and guided her ankle deep into the coldness. He pointed at Eric who eased in, laid out straight on his back, held his head and his plastic wrapped weapon up and let the river sweep him away. Lou waded in to his hips then waited for Mitch to escort Allie in deeper. Dean remained on guard until it was his turn.

Reading the indecision in her eyes, Mitch leaned close to her ear and asked on a soft whisper. "Do you swim?"

Allie shook her head. Tears welled in her eyes and for the first time since she'd been pulled from that van, he thought she might cry. He forced a smile hoping to ease her anxiety. Keeping his lips close to her ear, he whispered.

"Turn around, keep your back to me, knot your hands together on you chest and once we're in position, cross your ankles and keep your legs straight. Do your best to hold your head up and your mouth closed so you don't swallow too much water."

She did as commanded and gave him her back and placed her hands in a ball on her chest. Mitch positioned himself behind her, tucked his plastic wrapped weapon between them and wrapped his arms around her waist. With Lou's help, they eased back as one unit. Bodies tucked tightly together. Her head leveled with his chin. Her legs captured between his. The taut round bottom of hers nestled firmly against his pelvis was the only thing killing him on this ride. Cold water or not, his body reacted into a semi-hard condition he hoped she didn't notice.

For someone unable to swim, the way she molded into him amazed him. She relaxed allowing him full control. They rode the waterway like a fine tuned pair of body surfing professionals. Did that mean she trusted him? Mitch tightened his grip as they rounded a bend. When he leaned, she leaned. She mocked his every move and never released her ankles or her hands. She made it easy for him to guide them. They followed the bobbing head of Eric in the distance. Several miles of riding the water rush and he knew they needed to exit the cold before hypothermia set in. His men knew this as well. The lower they descended, the water slowed, making it easier to maneuver toward the bank. Mitch watched for Eric's lead. Seeing him wade ashore, Mitch guided them toward the shallows. As soon as possible, he stood lifting Allie to her feet.

She spun facing him, shoving her soaked hair back from her face as she sputtered, teeth chattering. "That was fun."

"Shush," Mitch reminded her the need for silence even though her delight thrilled him to the core. Allie nodded as she visibly shivered from head to toe. Cold settled into him as well, but he refused to acknowledge it. She needed warmth and fast.

Lou and Dean landed within a few feet of them. It didn't take much to communicate they desperately needed to get Allie dry. Her teeth rattled. She rubbed up and down her arms as she did a little dance in place. Mitch scooped her into his arms and carried her into the cover of the trees before anyone spotted them. Dean remained with him while Lou and Eric scouted for a place to recover and regroup their situation. Time ticked and seemed like hours before Eric returned. He motioned for them to follow. Less than a hundred feet from where they landed, a small village lay nestled at the base of the mountain.

Their reconnaissance found an empty house on the farthest end away from the water. Dinnertime smells filled the air making their stomachs growl. The village consisted of a total of fourteen houses in various sizes from the simple hut to the adobe type abodes with straw thatched roofs. One dirt road led into and out of the center. Beside two of the larger homes, ancient cars sat and looked as if they hadn't been driven in years. Due to the rain, no one milled about in the village. All seemed content to remain inside and dry.

Dry, Mitch huffed. That was one thing he wished he could make happen for Allie. Her lips were turning blue. Relief washed over him the moment they entered through the back door of the empty house. Heat filtered across his exposed skin and he heard Allie's audible sigh.

Lou had started a fire in the fireplace. There were only two windows and those were covered not allowing light from the fire to alert the outside world anyone was there. With the dark skies and heavy rain, Mitch doubted the smoke from the chimney would be noticed. The house was small with only three rooms, a kitchen/living area, a bedroom and a primitive bathroom. Lou stood from the fire and pointed toward the bathroom.

"There's running water, but no hot. I heated some over the fire for you." He smiled at Allie and Mitch's gut clenched. "It's not much, but it might help warm you up. Toss your clothes out here and I'll hang them to dry."

"Thanks," Allie managed to reply before Mitch clutched her elbow and guided her toward the bathroom. One look and he noticed there was no door. The bedroom didn't have one either. Great. Knowing she'd be naked in the tub again wrecked havoc on his resolve. But he knew she needed to soak in a warm tub to help relieve the cold from her system. If it were up to him, he'd slide in that old, claw-footed tub right along with her and help soothe her senses with a good dose of body heat. *His body heat.*

"Make it quick," Mitch stated in a much gruffer tone than he'd meant. "We've got to keep moving as soon as you're rested."

Mitch turned on his heels, marched into the bedroom and jerked the blanket off the makeshift mattress on the floor. He hung it haphazardly over the bathroom door granting Allie a smidgeon of privacy.

"Are you sure this place is secure?" Mitch turned to Lou.

"According to a letter I found, they've gone to visit their daughter and newborn grandbaby in Kosong."

Mitch read the note and was reassured the couple wouldn't return anytime soon. The letter informed them of the birth, which occurred two days prior. Knowing the Korean culture, they'd probably stay a month with their daughter to help, especially since it was her first child. *What would a child of theirs look like?* Where the hell had that come from? Mitch tossed the letter back on the table as he grappled for control over such ludicrous thoughts. Cold wet clothes landed at his feet. Turning he caught a glimpse of Allie's smile right before she closed the makeshift curtain. Every ounce of him hungered to cross that line between duty and desire. Mitch gathered her clothes and hung them to dry. *Think Marine. Think duty and nothing else.*

While Allie soaked, they stripped off their outer layers and hung them to dry around the fire. Each left on his camouflaged pants and tank top undershirts. They checked their weapons, ate, and then took their places. Lou sat at the back door. Dean took the front and Eric moved into the bedroom where one of the two windows was located.

Allie lowered over the edge of the small claw-footed tub. Instant heat warmed her toes, her calves, her thighs and then her bottom. Cupping the water in her hands, she brought the glorious heat to her face. Um, she sighed as she sank into the half-filled tub. Eyes closed, she envisioned a certain hunky Staff Sergeant and wished the situation were different. Why couldn't she have met him in a better place?

Because you live in two separate worlds. Allie's eyes sprang open wide. Would she see him again once this was over? God, she hoped so. But she lived a quite life working in a science lab at her father's side. And Mitch…he was a Marine whose life was filled with adventure. Sitting upright, she quickly ushered the water all over her body soothing the ache and the cold to ease. Before the water lost its allure, she stood and got out. There was no way she'd slow them down.

She grabbed a towel from the single shelf, wrapped it around her. Noticing it didn't cover much; she lifted the edge of the blanket and looked into the room. Mitch stood with his back to her. Lou sat leaning head back against a wall beside the back door and the other two were not in sight. As quick as possible, she lowered the blanket and wrapped it around her as well, leaving only her head visible.

The sight of him without his helmet, back turned to her standing in his undershirt, camo pants, and boots stole her breath. Sandy blond hair in a high and tight cut made her palms tingle with the urge to touch it. Was it soft? Broad shoulders stretched the green tank top taut. Biceps flexed as he removed MRE's—meals ready to eat—from a pack. Allie's mouth watered and she doubted it had anything to do with the food. When he lifted his gaze to hers, she swore her heart stopped for a millisecond. *Get a grip, Allie.* She reprimanded. *He's just doing his job nothing more.*

Mitch battled the urge to close the short distance between them and gather her in his arms. Allie looked like a lost angel wrapped in a blanket. Those big, brown eyes presented him with an invitation he couldn't accept. Her lips were no longer blue, but held a rich rosy hue begging him to taste. She was naked beneath that thin layer of cloth and that knowledge set his insides on fire. He swallowed hard and forced his voice to work and his libido to back down.

"Hungry?" He held an open container her way. "It's not much, but it'll take the edge off until we get you to safety."

Allie thanked him. Their fingers brushed as she accepted the meal. Heat sizzled up his arm to pool in his chest. He couldn't help but watch as she lowered to sit in front of the fire while she ate. The way her feet folded under her tush turned him on even more. The thin fabric caressed her skin like a glove, clinging to her luscious curves. Every ounce of blood in his system shifted to one location, causing a suddenly rock hard discomfort to strain against his pants.

"What about you and the others?"

Her question snapped him out of his dumbfounded, teenage crush-like stupor. Shaking his head, he regained a grasp on his senses. "We ate while you bathed."

"Then I won't take long," the sensual gaze she shot him across her shoulder nearly crumbled the fragile wall of restraint he had left. "I promise."

Forty minutes had past since they'd first entered the house and he knew they pressed their luck. Mitch turned, grabbed his shirt and dressed. The others followed suit. At least the inner layer was warm and dry. The outerwear still maintained a fine sheen of dampness, but it wasn't dripping anymore and at least it was warm on the inside. When he turned to hand Allie her semi-dry sweats, she wasn't by the fire. He spun on his heels and caught sight of her coming out of the bedroom. The man's shirt and pants gave her a tomboy appeal. The pants looked more like a pair of Capri's, which led him to believe the gentleman of the house was short. She carried a worn pair of boots. Before she stuck her foot inside, he handed her the pair of socks he'd grabbed earlier.

"Thought you might need these somewhere along the line, ma'am."

His consideration astounded her. The look in his eyes warmed her heart. He'd thought about her needs when she hadn't.

"Thank you." She managed to push past the knot in her throat and hoped he'd say something else in that rich Southern drawl. His accent tickled her ears and made her smile inwardly as a fleeting fantasy of him whispering sweetly ignited her soul.

The hidden promise within his eyes stated he was more than a Marine. He was a man in need of love. Allie broke their stare. *Stop,* she reprimanded. *Stop thinking of this as some sort of romantic venture.* Was she so desperate for adventure and excitement that she'd fantasize about her rescuer? Yeah, she huffed softly. She was. Years she'd spent in the lab with no one but her parents as companions. The two men she'd dated in her life were both boring drones. Neither had the gumption of this hunk of male species. Just looking at him caused her heart to pump faster.

Determination not to disappoint him or cause this mission to fail set in her gut. She knew she slowed them down and guessed in a normal operation they wouldn't have made this pit stop.

This was all because of her. From here forward, she planned to do whatever it took to help them get out of here in one piece. She shoved her feet into the boots and shimmied the rain poncho back on over her head. Digging deep she gathered her resolve and struggled to maintain a look of confidence, even though her nerves were strained and her muscles hurt.

The boots were snug, but she managed to walk well enough in them. They would do and it was better than running in bare feet. Eric slipped outside first. The others followed. A beat-up truck sat along the far wall of the house. Dean worked his magic and got the engine cranked. Lou drove. Allie sat in the middle, with Mitch at her side, weapon at the ready. Dean and Eric rode shotgun in the back.

They stayed on the dirt road only long enough to get within a mile of the location where they stowed the inflatable boat. The river still gave them the most direct and fastest route out of North

Korea. As far as Mitch was concerned, he wanted to get Allie out of there as fast as possible. Not sure if it were his imagination or not, he thought he heard the low rumble of quads in the distance. His gut told him, Kwan hadn't given up.

Body surfing down the tributary may have gotten them ahead by a few miles, but it didn't mean they were safe. They'd lost valuable time by stopping to let Allie rest. He shot a sideways glance her way. She still looked tired, but at least she no longer shivered from head to toe. He lingered longer than he should have on her lips, before he dragged his gaze back to scanning for the enemy. Lou maneuvered the truck as far as it could go along the rough terrain off road. Then they hoofed it to the boat. Running full force as the drone of engines closed in on them.

Within seconds, Eric and Dean uncovered the boat and started the motor. Mitch helped Allie in and ordered her to crouch in the center. They hadn't gone far when something whizzed past

Mitch's head. They were under fire. Lou began evasive maneuvers. Mitch, Eric and Dean took combat positions and prepared to return fire on Mitch's command. Normally they were in and out, no shots fired unless fired upon. That was the way of the Force Recon Marine. Repeatedly, shots came close but failed to reach them. They were out of range.

Something in Mitch's gut told him it wasn't over. They wouldn't stop there.

Dark skies and continuous rain provided a cover of near invisibility for the Americans as they forged down river headed for the sanctity of the Demilitarized zone and the safety of South Korea. Allie kept crouched low in the middle of the boat as he asked. He and the others provided a wall of protection, but none would be a complete shield in the eye of a well-placed sharpshooter. Mitch's chest tightened. Soon they'd reach the one area of the river they were most vulnerable. The last half mile of North Korean territory consisted of steep cliffs on both sides and nowhere to hide.

Kwan wasn't stupid. If he planned an ambush, that would be the most logical location. At least in Mitch's trained mind, it seemed the best. All he could hope was they didn't have the capabilities to out run them and get ahead of their high-speed boat. Every muscle tightened the moment they entered the cliffs. Mitch scanned the upper regions for any sign of life.

Nothing. But he didn't relax. He wouldn't relax until the package had been delivered to safe ground. The package, he huffed. Swallowing hard, he couldn't completely convince himself to think of her as a package. She had a nice package he wished he could unwrap and explore. Visions of her naked form danced behind his eyes tormenting his self-control. It had only been a glimpse, but it had been enough to ignite a burning curiosity he couldn't deny.

When this was over, he truly needed to rethink his decision of living a life alone. He lifted his night vision goggles to give his eyes a rest. Glancing at her, he knew those big, brown eyes stared his way even though he couldn't see her. He could feel the heat of her stare. Not condescending, not judgmental…simply sensual, which shocked him to the core. What would a woman of her stature, her intelligence want with a man like him? She had a family, a life and a career. And he, Mitch sighed sliding the goggles back in place. He came from nothing, had nothing and lived for only one reason…to serve as a Marine.

The goggles were barely in place when he caught sight of a movement in the distance high on the far bank. A quick adjustment zoomed in on the area. From where they were, he couldn't get a fix on what they were doing, but he sensed it wasn't good. A spark and a trail of smoke widened his eyes.

"Incoming," he yelled causing Lou to counter the attack with an evasive maneuver. The grenade landed several hundred feet short, sending a wave of water hustling after them. The wave hit with a solid force. Lou's skill had them riding it with the ease of a surfboarder.

"The border's in sight," Dean called out, pointing at the lighted compound.

Twin guard towers stood on either side of the waterway entrance. He knew they'd been spotted by the sudden flash of strong beams of light on the river. It lit up their position as if it were daylight. Damn, might as well draw a bull's-eye on their backs. They just had to cross under the fence and they'd be safe. A shrill whistling in the air snapped his head back around to see another missile-fired, grenade headed their way. This had more stamina and seemed like it wouldn't miss. Must've been shot from an RPG-7, he mused right before it hit the water within ten feet of them.

"Brace yourselves," Mitch screamed as he turned, dove, and wrapped himself around Allie.

A solid wall of water lifted the boat six feet into the air, tossing it end over end like a toy. As the boat flipped so did the well-prepared Marines. Lou, Eric, and Dean entered at angles, which landed them closer to the safety zone. Mitch and Allie hit the water curled in a ball of bodies. Seconds past with no sight of them. Lou dove first, followed by the other two. Frantically, they searched battling powerful currents and limited visual.

Mitch hit bottom, twisted, loosening his legs from around Allie then shoved off propelling them upward. He guided them to the surface. The sound of her gasp when they broke the top sent relief crashing through his system. They hit the water and went under so fast, he didn't get the chance to tell her to take a deep breath and hold it. But she was smarter than that, he laughed at himself. Common sense made a person hold their breath before going under. It was a natural reflex to prevent drowning.

"You okay," he managed to gasp over the roar of the river as he held her in the rescue swimmer position. Her back pressed to his chest, his arm under hers around her chest while he maintained buoyancy for the both of them.

"Yeah." She tilted her chin trying to see his face as she added, "You okay?"

Having him wrapped around her equaled ecstasy in her book. The coldness of the water gave her a momentary shock when they first hit, but she managed to capture enough air in her lungs to survive. Sinking deeper and deeper, her heart raced, but she refused to succumb to fear. Mitch had a hold on her and she knew he wouldn't let her drown. It seemed like forever before he brought them to the surface. They had been fired upon and nearly killed, but he saved her again. Cradled in those strong arms gave her the confidence to relax in the water even though she didn't know how to swim.

In her position, she spotted the others before Mitch did. Unable to do anything else for fear of causing an issue in their progress, she gave a loud sharp whistle, hoping to catch their attention. Lou spotted them and motioned to the others. Once they regrouped, they swam for the border. Allie kicked her legs in an effort to help speed the motion.

Cold seeped into her bones and she prayed she'd never be this wet again. Powerful stokes brought them closer and closer. Bright lights shone on them. Voices called out in foreign tongues. It surprised her when Mitch replied. He spoke Korean. Lou, Eric and Dean crossed through the fenced gate that the border patrol opened. They lifted from the water and stood on the dock Mitch and she brought up the rear. They were a few feet away from crossing the line when the water exploded behind them.

Mitch curled in a ball gloving around her as if forming another layer of skin for her protection. He tucked her head under his as they tumbled over and over through the giant wave. They bounced from one object to another like a ball in a pinball game. The mound of muscle that was Mitch softened the repercussion of the blows. Several feet inside the safety zone, they washed up on shore just passed the docks.

Lou reached them first. The sound of his voice called to her from somewhere far off tugging her back to consciousness.

"Miss Summers, Mitch can you hear me?"

Seconds ticked away before she pried her eyes open. On a hefty bout of coughing, she cleared the water from her lungs and grappled for air. Mitch didn't move. His eyes were closed.

"Mitch," she gasped.

He didn't respond.

"Mitch, man can you hear me?" Lou said as he tried to pry his buddy from around Allie.

Even unconscious he still protected her. His breathing seemed almost non-existent. Tears streamed down her cheeks. Over and over, she called his name to no avail. Eric, Dean and several medics for the Marine Corps ran to their aid. It took three men to unwrap Mitch's arms and legs from around Allie.

On hands and knees she crawled to his outstretched body. *Please, God, Please let him live,* she prayed.

"His vitals are weak." One of the medics stated.

"Let's get him inside." The other replied.

Allie struggled to her feet as they placed him on a stretcher. Lou grasped her elbow and wrapped an arm around her waist right before her knees buckled. Lifting her gaze to his, she commanded on a graveled breath.

"He's got to live."

"Mitch is strong. He'll make it."

"He has to."

Exhaustion controlled her system as her legs weakened and her eyes closed. Nothing mattered to her but Mitch.

Chapter Four

Six weeks later State side.

Sergeant Lou Randle entered the hospital room. As it had been every day for the past six weeks, she sat at Mitch's side. She shot a weak smile across her shoulder at him and stood. He nodded in acknowledgement.

"Any progress?" Lou asked.

"No, but I'm sure he'll come around any day now." Allie replied.

She leaned over the man in the bed, kissed his brow and then whispered in his ear. Turning on her heels, she gathered her things and headed for the door.

"You do that every time." Lou smiled. "What do you tell him?"

"My Christmas wish," Allie said. "I won't be here tomorrow, Sergeant Randle. It's Christmas

Eve and I promised to share the time with my Father. But, I will return to spend Christmas Day with Mitch."

Lou touched her elbow. "He's a lucky man to have a woman like you."

Allie looked over her shoulder at her wounded soldier. Medical tests showed no definitive answer to why he lay unconscious. The doctor claimed his body had taken such an extreme beating it seemed his system had gone into some sort of dormant state to recuperate. Broken ribs and a bruised lung would heal in time. Would the rest of him? She swallowed hard hoping for the best. Sadness filled her soul. She'd met the perfect man and didn't know what she'd do if she lost him before they got the chance to explore the feelings ignited between them.

"It doesn't look like he's got anyone else. No ones ever come to see him except us and the other Marines in your group. Doesn't he have family?"

"No ma'am." Lou shook his head. "Mitch grew up an orphan. He entered the Marines right out of high school. We're the closest to family he's ever known."

Tears threatened to fall but she blinked them back. Mitch was alone. She glanced at him and smiled. Not anymore. No matter what happened, he had her.

"Watch over him for me," Allie stared at Lou. "Merry Christmas Sergeant Randle."

"Merry Christmas, Miss Summers." Lou paused, then added as she stepped into the hallway. "If you need anything, please don't hesitate to ask. I'm at your beck and call, anytime of night or day."

"Thank you, I'll keep that in mind."

Lou stood and watched her walk down the hall then turned back towards the bed. As soon as he reached the bedside, a graveled voice grabbed and held his attention in awe.

"You hitting on my woman, Sergeant."

"Ohmygod, you're awake. Let me catch her."

Mitch caught his wrist before he could move. It took a great effort, but he managed to turn his head, open his eyes and continue.

"I've got a better idea." He took a deep breath, licked his lips then added. "But I'm going to need your help to pull it off."

* * * * * *

Allie took the last tray of cookies from the oven and placed them on the cooling racks. It was the third batch of gingerbread men she'd made that resembled Marines. Oh God, who did she have on her mind? This was the first time in five weeks she hadn't sat at his side, talking to him, reading a book or newspaper to him, praying he'd wake. With a shake of her head, she truly didn't need an answer. She knew it was the one and only Sergeant Mitch Sinclair who'd won her heart and soul.

The ring of the doorbell snapped her from another daydream of the hunky Marine. She issued a silent prayer for his safekeeping and well being as she exited the kitchen and crossed the living room. Her father descended the stairs as she reached the front door.

Swinging it open, her heart skipped a beat and her jaw dropped. Dress blues never looked so good. From his head to his toes, he stood regal and strong in appearance. One would never have known he'd lain in a dormant state for the past weeks. Sword at his side, gold buttons shined and his white hat positioned shadowing what she knew were a set of gorgeous brilliant blue eyes. She couldn't speak for fear she may be suffering from some sort of delusion and he'd disappear the moment she said a word.

His words came loud and clear on his thick southern drawl touching her heart and sealing her fate.

"I understand someone in this house asked for a special gift for Christmas."

Allie's voice shook. "How…how are you here? When I left you last night, you were unconscious."

She wanted to touch him, but kept her hands knotted in her apron. If she reached for him, would he dissipate and this turned out to be a mere dream. She wasn't sure she could handle such a grand disappointment. The last few weeks were tough, between trekking to the hospital daily, to taking care of father, to dealing with loving an unconscious man and not knowing if she'd ever see the wondrous shade of blue again. Everything weighed heavy on her spirit and soul, but it was a sliver of hope that kept her going. If this was a dream, God, she prayed she'd never wake.

"I had a little help getting here." Following the direction of his nod, she noticed Sergeant Randle leaned against a car in the driveway. Odd, she hadn't seen him earlier, but her eyesight had been narrowed by a vision from heaven that filled her doorway.

"Oh my God, it is you." Allie fell into his arms, crying and laughing at the same time. Her prayers were answered. "This isn't a dream."

Mitch cupped her chin, lifting her gaze to meet his. "I'm here because of you. Everyday, a sweet voice whispered to my tired soul. It was you who guided me back and gave me the strength to heal."

He ran his thumb across her trembling lip and brushed the hair from her eyes.

"Allie, it was your Christmas wish that touched my heart and led me to you. I heard your voice everyday. You were there for me when I needed someone in my life the most. I couldn't let you down."

Allie swallowed hard against the lump in her throat and stated on a shaky whisper. "All I want for Christmas is a Marine."

Mitch leaned in close, gathered her in his arms and smiled, hovering within millimeters of her lips and stated right before he captured her mouth in a passionate embrace.

"Wish granted."

About the Author

Tara Nina creates in a variety of ranges from steamy hot to simmering sweet, which includes paranormals, contemporaries, suspense and sci-fi. She's a Southerner living in the northern wilds of New Jersey complete with grown children, four dogs, six turtles and a mountain man for a husband.

She loves to hear from readers so feel free to contact her via email tara@taranina.com

Please don't get discouraged if it takes a little while before she responds. Unfortunately, she hasn't hit the lottery yet and has to work to battle the bills of home ownership. Being a full-time writer is on her bucket list and one day, she hopes to achieve that goal.

Join her Clan MacKinnon Fan Club/Newsletter for updates on what's new and exciting in her world. http://taranina.com/join-the-clan/
Check out her website http://taranina.com
She is also available on the following media outlets:
Facebook:
https://www.facebook.com/TaraNinaAuthor
Twitter: https://twitter.com/taranina
Pinterest: https://www.pinterest.com/taranina/

Books by Tara Nina

Cursed MacKinnon's series:

Curse of the Gargoyle (book 1)

Eyes of Stone (book 2)

Cursed Laird (book 3)

Haunted Laird (book 4)

Mountain Men: Brothers Dupree ~ Trilogy

Mindwarp

www.ingramcontent.com/pod-product-compliance
Lightning Source LLC
Chambersburg PA
CBHW020141150626
46552CB00021B/1232